WiLLOW

AVA GUSTAFSON

WISE Ink
CREATIVE ★ PUBLISHING

ISBN 13: 978-1-945769-12-2

Library of Congress Catalog Number: 2016913217
Printed in the United States of America
First Printing: 2016
20   19   18   17   16   5   4   3   2   1

Cover and interior design by Kelly McManus, McManus Creative, Inc.

Wise Ink Creative Publishing
837 Glenwood Avenue
Minneapolis, MN 55405
www.wiseinkpub.com

To order, visit www.thewillowseries.com or call (734)-426-6248. Reseller discounts available.

Dedicated To:

My Beautiful Jesus, for giving me the Word(s)

Kym Christopherson, for helping me see my dream.

Joyce Meyer, for teaching me how to
"develop my character"

... and to YOU, who read and enjoy this story ...

Continue to Love, to Give and to Share with
a Joyful & Grateful heart!

Galatians 5:22

To see how your purchase of this book is helping others, check out Willow's Whispers at www.thewillowseries.com

Weeping willow is what they call me,

I don't know why for I do not weep.

By the river and under the stars,
to the sound of water is how I sleep.

Mama raccoon and her babies
like to play by the light of the moon.
They scurry away while I'm dreaming.

A new day will be here soon.

Dragonflies joyfully wake me, singing

and dancing around my head.

Birds chirp softly, shaking their feathers.

In a flash
they fly out of bed.

Squirrels run up and down me playing a game of hide-and-seek.
They invite turtle to join the game,

though they know he likes to peek.

Water lilies ripple
as they float on the riverbed's top.

They make a perfect path
for all the little frogs to hop.

The water quenches my thirst as it splashes.
I dip my toes to take a drink.

Breezy ribbons stroke my branches.

Their soft caresses make me think.

Maybe they think I'm lonely growing here along the shore,

but I have friends who love me
and friends that I adore.

joy

love

peace

patience

kindness

faithfullness

goodness

gentleness

self control

I know each day is beautiful,
it's wonderful and good....so give and share
and love each other, as we know we should.

love
peace
joy
kindness
faithfulness
self-control

They call me weeping willow,
but I'm a happy willow tree
and the light that shines within me glows...

... for all the world to see!

The Roots of Willow

Willow was a childhood dream that lay dormant into my adult years, until she whispered to me during a visualization session of yoga. Willow has been nurtured and pruned with the help of my husband, family and friends, who encouraged me to expand on a small inspired poem. Thanks to Katrina's gifts and talents, Willow now springs to life, out of my dreams and on to the pages of this book, in full color to share with the world. Sprouting out soon ..."Willow's New Friend".

AVA GUSTAFSON, Author

Ava Gustafson lives in a modest home in Spooner, WI with her husband, Randy and her four legged furry friends. She is a lover of Jesus and the simple things in life. It is her dream for her books to branch out into many homes and hands, touching peoples lives and helping develop children's hearts.

"Happiness isn't something that depends on our surroundings ... It's something we make inside ourselves."
— Corrie ten Boom

KATRINA DOHM, Illustrator

44 years ago, Katrina's kindergarten teacher shared that this creative child would do something in the area of art! After sharing her passion as an art teacher for 22 years, Katrina Dohm has recently discovered that she was put out on this earth to help people make their dreams come true...

"All of your dreams can come true if you have the courage to pursue them."
— Walt Disney

I Could Not Have Done It With Out YOU!

FOR YOUR HELP AND SUPPORT ... BOTTOMLESS THANKS TO:

Randy Gustafson, Katrina Dohm, Julie Silcott Roberts,

Sabra & Vince Vacca, Kathleen Duffy Silcott, James Silcott,

Joyce & Pat Savage, Satsuki Scoville & Family, Randy & Mary King,

Ross Browne, Erika Gorian, Kim Landry-Ayres, Kym Christopherson,

Barbara Johnson, Jeff & Linda McIntyre, Carol Folk,

Jerry & Debbie Thompson, Dorothy Kniseley, Christy & Tom Sarne,

Bonnie Niemi, Amber & Aaron Anderson, Anonymous,

Michele & Jason Martell (Pine Brook Farm), Cindy & John Kirn,

Jeff Dietrich (NWRPC) Kellie Hultgren, Emily Rodvold, Kelly McManus,

Jerry Friends (Thomson Shore Distribution), Shannon Peterman Photography

and last, but certainly not least ... Dara Beevas & Wise Ink.

May your kindness and generosity come back to you ten fold!